Samuel French Acting Edition

Two of Us

by Ross Howard

SAMUELFRENCH.COM   SAMUELFRENCH.CO.UK

FOR PRODUCTION ENQUIRIES

UNITED STATES AND CANADA
Info@SamuelFrench.com
1-866-598-8449

UNITED KINGDOM AND EUROPE
Plays@SamuelFrench.co.uk
020-7255-4302

Each title is subject to availability from Samuel French, depending upon country of performance. Please be aware that *TWO OF US* may not be licensed by Samuel French in your territory. Professional and amateur producers should contact the nearest Samuel French office or licensing partner to verify availability.

MUSIC USE NOTE

Licensees are solely responsible for obtaining formal written permission from copyright owners to use copyrighted music in the performance of this play and are strongly cautioned to do so. If no such permission is obtained by the licensee, then the licensee must use only original music that the licensee owns and controls. Licensees are solely responsible and liable for all music clearances and shall indemnify the copyright owners of the play(s) and their licensing agent, Samuel French, against any costs, expenses, losses and liabilities arising from the use of music by licensees. Please contact the appropriate music licensing authority in your territory for the rights to any incidental music.

IMPORTANT BILLING AND CREDIT REQUIREMENTS

If you have obtained performance rights to this title, please refer to your licensing agreement for important billing and credit requirements.

TWO OF US received a staged reading at Southwark Playhouse in London on February 26, 2015. The play was directed by Ross Howard and produced by Jayne Dickinson and Jennifer Bryden. The cast was as follows:

SHE	Alexis Sun
HE	Jeff Mash
SARAH	Christy Meyer
ROBERT	Trevor White
GUN STORE / HUSBAND / PHOTOGRAPHER	John Schwab
JUDE / SUNNY / WIFE	Alexandra Metaxa

TWO OF US was produced by New Light Theater Project as part of the Ross Howard Festival at Access Theater in New York City on October 19, 2016. The production was directed by Sarah Norris, with set design by Brian Dudkiewicz, costume design by Genevieve V. Beller, lighting design by Michael O'Connor, and sound design by Andy Evan Cohen. The stage manager was Erikka Anderson. The cast was as follows:

SHE	Vivian Chiu
HE	Chris Bert
SARAH	Janae Mitchell
ROBERT	Christopher Daftsios
GUN STORE / HUSBAND / PHOTOGRAPHER	Dan Fenaughty
JUDE / SUNNY / WIFE	Lea Mckenna-Garcia

CHARACTERS

There are ten characters that can be played by a minimum cast of six actors:

SHE – Female. Around thirty. Japanese-American. Known from now in the script as "Gloria."

HE – Male. Her husband. Mid-twenties. From Decatur, Georgia. Has the accent.

SARAH – Female. From the Gospel of Peter. Wife of Abraham, mother of Isaac. Exudes the urgency of the reformed and the redeemed.

ROBERT – Male. Chief Adviser to He. A man of disguises with the skill of a matador.

JUDE – Female. Mid-twenties, a regular "lurker" around the Dakota apartment building in New York City.

HONOLULU GUN STORE – Male. A walking, talking gun store personified.

SUNNY – Female. A prostitute. Eastern European. Played by actor playing Jude.

HUSBAND – Male. Played by actor playing Honolulu Gun Store.

WIFE – Female. Played by actor playing Jude and Sunny.

PHOTOGRAPHER – Male. Late thirties, photographer outside the Dakota apartment building. From New Jersey. Played by actor playing Honolulu Gun Store and Husband.

SETTING

The play is set in the warmth of Honolulu and in a cold December in New York City, 1980.

A design which illustrates the stark contrast of these two locations, either literally or metaphorically, is encouraged.

Under no circumstances must the music of John Lennon or The Beatles be used.

"...and the torrent burst against it and immediately it collapsed, and the ruin of that house was very great."

– Luke 6:49

Genesis

GLORIA. He told me he wanted to go all the way around the world.

Those were the first words he ever said to me.

I said I'd do what I could to help.

I did a lot more because I liked him and he liked me.

There were times he would just appear at my work...

> (**HE** *appears in a spotlight.* **HE** *is wearing a Hawaiian shirt, sunglasses, and a lei hangs around his neck.* **HE** *is smiling and holding a takeout breakfast tray with two cups of coffee and two pastries. There is also a single red rose sticking out of his shirt pocket.*)

HE. Hey, good lookin'.

What's cookin'?

GLORIA. I told my colleague Heather at the travel agency, "I think my client has a thing for me."

He was generous and intelligent, kind and gentle...

a little goofy perhaps...his stories, his missionary work, I was in awe of him, and he was cute.

He was so cute.

HE. So what time are you free later?

Okay. I'll pick you up then.

> (**HE** *takes a coffee and pastry for himself and offers the tray and rose. Lights fade on* **HE.**)

GLORIA. When he went away across the globe,

for that long six weeks, he would send me letters.

I liked the way he wrote. I saw good traits in his handwriting.

That was one of the things that made me trust him

and I counted the days until he came back.

From then on we were inseparable the two of us.

My doorbell would go late at night and it would always
be him.

He said that I was kind and that I never turned him
away,

but the truth was I never wanted to go to bed or be left
alone

if I knew he was close. I always wanted him to just
come in,

sit down with me, or lie with me and talk.

1. Honolulu – March 1980

(**HE** *enters wearing the same Hawaiian shirt as earlier, but he appears less presentable. He wears regular glasses now and is holding a large, thick, and well-worn book. He sits at the kitchen table, he smells the book, inhaling deeply, and then begins rapidly flicking through the pages with relish, but to where he can't be really reading much at all.* **GLORIA** *enters and is initially startled by* **HE***'s presence. The underlying nature of communication between* **GLORIA** *and* **HE** *is frequently one of impatience rather than outright acrimony.*)

GLORIA. Where were you?

HE. I came in through the fire escape.

GLORIA. Where've you been? Your mom just left.

HE. You don't say? Well good timing.

Yeah, I know. I saw.

GLORIA. So you saw each other?

HE. I saw her. She didn't see me.

GLORIA. She's *your* mom. She was very disappointed.

Very disappointed that you didn't show.

We even got a pie.

HE. You got a pie?

GLORIA. Have some.

Blueberry pie.

It's delicious.

HE. From where?

GLORIA. Feretti's. Go on. We saved some for you.

HE. She paid, right?

GLORIA. I don't remember.

HE. Think?

Think Gloria.

Who paid for the pie?

GLORIA. Your mom.

Your mom paid for the pie.

HE. Okay.

Did you offer to pay for the pie?

I know what you're like.

GLORIA. I might've.

Honestly, I don't remember.

HE. Well, it's important, Gloria.

We need to consolidate. Remember?

What we don't need we don't have,

get it out of the house.

Just a clean break.

GLORIA. It's just a pie.

HE. It's not the point. It's the principle.

It's not just a pie. We shouldn't be decadent.

We've been just too loose for too long.

(Silence.)

GLORIA. I saw you threw out my blender.

HE. We don't need it.

GLORIA. It helps me mix stuff. To blend...stuff.

HE. I didn't throw out the spoons, did I?

We have big wooden spoons, right?

They're still here.

GLORIA. Sure.

HE. It'll build up your arms anyway.

Give them some definition.

Besides, I'll be here a lot more now.

I can do a lot of the food preparation.

So I quit my job today.

GLORIA. Oh! Why?

HE. Because I despair of the people in that place.

GLORIA. You despair of everyone.

You shouldn't take such things to heart.

Everybody has somebody at work they hate.

HE. I didn't say hate, Gloria.

I despair.

That's what I said.

A pigeon flew through the kitchen window.

GLORIA. Huh?

HE. At work.

GLORIA. Oh.

HE. You're jumpy.

You should have seen the poor thing, Gloria.

It flapped and flapped and circled...

and with the steam coming up from

the vats it just didn't know what to do,

where to go, or where it was.

GLORIA. Poor pigeon.

HE. I'm serious.

All the migrants started laughing,

and then some bright spark stopped peeling,

put down his knife and started throwing the potatoes

that'd gone real bad. Throwing them right at the bird.

Then it was like dominoes, everyone started doing it

and before you knew it...scores of these rotten potatoes

were flying at it, Gloria. Like...like bombs!

I prayed for the pigeon, that it would just get away

and I yelled for them to stop but they wouldn't.

Then someone threw a ripe potato and knocked it

clean out.

GLORIA. That's awful.

HE. I could hardly look. He was like he'd won the lottery.

He went over, picked it up, holding it aloft,

feathers dropping like snow, then with a grin as wide as the

beach outside, chopped the bird's head clean off.

And all people could do was cheer and laugh like a bunch of hyenas.

So yeah, I quit my job.

    (A beat.)

GLORIA. *(Demanding.)* And?

    (Silence.)

What are we going to do now?

How are we gonna –

HE. Relax. Don't panic. You keep your job.

We got the money owed to us for the Dali plaque coming in. I don't know, maybe we sell the Rockwell print.

We can get ten for that easy.

GLORIA. But you wanted to be a collector.

That's what you said you wanted.

HE. Yeah, well, things change, Gloria.

I'll stay here and be a house husband.

You know, cook, clean.

Take charge of the day-to-day running of the household.

GLORIA. I don't want you here on your own for hours on end.

It's not good for you.

HE. Well this is it. I can go to the library. Take walks.

I won't run myself into the ground here. I promise.

But you won't have to do anything around here.

We'd be a real team and get back on track.

I was in the library today after I left work, and I've given this

some real thought... I think if I really worked at it, on my breaks...

from the work around here...if I really disciplined myself, I could

read everything they have in there.

GLORIA. You'd read all the books in Honolulu Public Library?

HE. All the books. Every single one.

It's not a big library. I've seen a lot bigger.

A lot bigger. Just think of all that knowledge acquired, Gloria.

I bet nobody's ever done that. Read a whole library.

I'd just make my way through. Book by book, shelf by shelf, aisle by aisle.

Just think what can happen from doing that.

Where that could all lead for the two of us.

The possibilities. It'll be useful for both of us down the long stretch...who knows what we can be.

(*A beat.*)

What?

GLORIA. I don't want you putting yourself back to the way –

HE. Don't worry.

GLORIA. ...Where you were.

HE. Don't even worry about that.

This is precisely why I want to do this.

Precisely why, Gloria.

I can't live working in a kitchen, peeling potatoes, watching people slaughter birds, wearing shirts with my name embroidered on the pocket.

GLORIA. I want you to feel better about things, I do, but –

HE. I know you doubt me.

GLORIA. Oh I don't doubt you!

(*A beat.*)

Look at me.

(*A beat.*)

GLORIA. Look at me.

HE. What?

GLORIA. I don't doubt you.

I love you, but you go from one thing to another.

There are times, where I just can't keep up with you.

HE. I know how it sounds but we just need more order is all.

Less chaos. Stuff gets to – things get too...chaotic.

I can't stand it. And when I was in the library today it just

hit me like a bolt of lightning. We need a system or something.

For our lives. Our marriage. The whole slam.

Just something reliable, you know. Like a code.

Like a Dewey Decimal System mode of living

or something.

GLORIA. I don't even know what that means.

HE. We just need to get organized.

    (Silence.)

GLORIA. Your mom was talkative tonight.

HE. You don't say.

    (A beat.)

So how is she?

GLORIA. She's...how she always is.

    (A beat.)

She thinks we should start a family.

    (Silence.)

HE. Is she still seeing that kid?

GLORIA. Oh, he's not a kid.

HE. He's like twenty-six!

GLORIA. That's not a kid.

HE. I'm twenty-five!

GLORIA. She's happy. Why can't you be happy for her?

I thought that's what you wanted.

Why you helped her come out here.

HE. I didn't bring her out here for that, Gloria.

Jeez, I get her a lawyer, I move her here,

I got her a job at Sears, helped her look for a place...

I didn't bring her here to...to pimp her on the beach!

What?

GLORIA. She's not a prostitute.

HE. Why are you on her side all of a sudden?

You hated her when she first got here.

GLORIA. I did not hate her!

HE. All you did was complain! You wanted her out!

You want her to move back in now? Is that it?

GLORIA. No.

HE. She's here all the freakin' time!

I can't breathe! Every day you asked me when she
was gonna find her own place, when was she leaving
and now what, you're best buddies all of a sudden?

She's coming around for pie on a Tuesday?

What do you talk about?

GLORIA. Who?

HE. You and my mom.

What do you talk about?

GLORIA. We just talk!

HE. Her guys?

GLORIA. We talk about everything.

You. Everything.

HE. Oh gimme a break, she talks about nothing but herself.

GLORIA. That's not true. She asks –

HE. She given you one good reason why she won't let my
sister come out here and live with her?

GLORIA. Your sister is too young for here. She's seventeen.

HE. And that's your opinion?

GLORIA. Well, I think she's right.

HE. You know why, don't you?
   She'll be in the way, that's why.
   Spoil her good time.
   Spoil her "new life."
   You wanna be like her?
   You wanna be like that –

GLORIA. Stop this now!
   What's gotten into you?

> *(Silence. They glare at each other for a tense moment.* **HE** *apologetically gets up and embraces her.)*

HE. I'm sorry, baby. I'm sorry.
   It's just been a rough day. I'm sorry
   I love you.

GLORIA. *(Pushing* **HE** *away.)* Get away from me.
   I'm gonna take a bath.

> *(A beat.)*

Eat some pie.

> *(***GLORIA*** *exits.* **HE** *returns slowly to the table and slumps down at it.* **HE** *looks around the room.* **HE** *goes back briefly to flicking through the pages of his book but his attention soon wanders.* **ROBERT** *enters. Until specified otherwise he is dressed in a black suit and tie and wears a bowler hat. He has the look of a Victorian London banker and speaks like one.)*

ROBERT. You called for me, sir.

HE. I did?

ROBERT. Why yes, I got here as soon as I could.

HE. Uh, sure...did...did I give a reason?

ROBERT. The telegram was not specific but I assume it's fiscal.
   I gather you have had quite a day.

(**HE** *sits up and assumes a somewhat officious
position.*)

HE. Uh, yeah.

(*A beat.*)

Yes. Indeed.

I do need your help.

ROBERT. As ever, it is an honour to serve.

HE. You may have heard I quit my job today.

ROBERT. If I may say so, sir, you had every right to do so.
The pigeon incident left you with no choice.

HE. No choice. Thank you.

ROBERT. I mean, gosh.

HE. I know.

ROBERT. It is not good for you to be around such barbarity.

HE. So you understand?

ROBERT. Gloria will too. In time.

HE. It's for the best.
I wouldn't have done it otherwise.
Everything I do is for me and her.
For the two of us.

ROBERT. You've always been our leader.
We have nothing but faith.

HE. That's good to hear.
But my quitting, staying here, at home...
what effect will this have on our economy?

ROBERT. Well, sir. We are still at the same state of play
since the last review.

HE. Yes, the dossier.
You have it for me?

ROBERT. I can summarize.

HE. Sure.

(**HE** *leans forward in his chair.*)

ROBERT. Foremost, the credit card debts need to be addressed.

Interest on your Visa card has spiraled and the artwork you bought...

HE. I've already told Gloria we will sell those –

ROBERT. You will have to.

HE. I will.

ROBERT. A speedy sale on both items is crucial to steady the ship.

After that, cutting your cloth accordingly should see you pay

any outstanding balance.

HE. Good. Right, but most important.

Gloria's paycheck being our sole revenue...

ROBERT. With discipline there is no reason that you cannot keep the apartment. With Gloria's monthly input

we have deduced that after all mandatory expenses,

you will have around one hundred dollars a month remaining

to live on.

HE. A hundred dollars?

Will that be enough?

ROBERT. You will have to change the way you have been living up until now

but it is more than possible, yes.

Eating out, for example.

The fancy restaurants and so forth,

I'm afraid that will have to be seldom to never.

HE. We can do that.

ROBERT. No, you can't.

HE. I know, I mean we can do that.

ROBERT. No, that's what I'm telling you.

You can't continue to do that.

HE. No, I know. I meant we can do that.

As in not doing that anymore.

ROBERT. Oh forgive me. My fault. Yes, renting Lincoln Continentals, spending getaway weekends on Waikiki Beach and staying at the Moana Hotel, that can no longer be allowed to happen.

The episodic spending and pleasure sprees that the two of you may have grown accustomed...

it is just not feasible. Not under the new agenda.

HE. I understand.

ROBERT. Is there anything else?

HE. How about cultural policy. Where do we stand?

ROBERT. The senate has applauded your decision to read all the books

in the Honolulu Public Library. It will be no mean feat. A most ambitious program.

HE. Yes, but I believe necessary.

For the development of our state.

ROBERT. Absolutely. We suggest one thing.

HE. What's that?

ROBERT. You begin with the travel section.

HE. I was going to start with philosophy.

ROBERT. Sir, if I can be so bold...

HE. Yes?

ROBERT. Perhaps communicate with Gloria on a far less adversarial level

than you are at the moment. A shared interest will do wonders

for the stability of the Union. Read Travel. Just a suggestion.

She is a travel agent after all. Support for what she does has never been

so important. You must not leave her feeling stranded. She is our foundation.

> (**GLORIA** *enters with a towel around her. She watches* **HE**, *who has his back turned to her and is leaning forward. She does not acknowledge* **ROBERT**.)

HE. Is that the senate's view or just yours?

>   *(No response.)*

   I will consider it.

ROBERT. Ooh, sir! Another thing...

HE. Yes.

ROBERT. If I can go one step further in the bold department...

GLORIA. Hey, have you seen my –?

>   *(No response.* **HE** *is still engaged with* **ROBERT.***)*

HE. *(To* **ROBERT.***)* Sure. Your counsel is appreciated.

GLORIA. I'm just –

ROBERT. Enjoy yourself. Try to relax. Books are fun.
   Revisit that escapism of childhood
   when you can.
   Reconnect with those old acquaintances, those old joys.

HE. I will.

ROBERT. The old comforts.
   Indulge that young boy inside of you.

HE. Sure.

ROBERT. That little child inside the man.

HE. Yes, good.

ROBERT. THAT is just as important.

>   *(Pause.)*

   Are we adjourned?

HE. Sure.

ROBERT. Forgive me, sir. My wife is in labour with our third...
   just to explain my haste.

HE. Oh, uhm...congratulations...
   and good luck.

ROBERT. Until next time.

>   *(***ROBERT*** *exits.)*

GLORIA. You okay?

HE. Hey, did you pick up toilet paper?

GLORIA. Yes.

> (**HE** *exits abruptly.* **SARAH** *enters.* **GLORIA** *is dumbstruck.*)

Holy shit! Who are you?

> (**SARAH** *smiles warmly at* **GLORIA.** *A moment of silence between them.*)

SARAH. I'm Sarah.

GLORIA. Sarah?

> (*A beat.*)

As in wife of Abraham, mother of Isaac.

SARAH. Well, if you're gonna boil it down.

GLORIA. What...er...why...what...

> (*Offering at least something.*)

...brings you to Hawaii?

SARAH. You, Gloria. You.

Glorious Gloria.

GLORIA. Oh stop!

I'm not so glorious.

I just got in from work and I'm all sweaty.

I was just going to take a bath.

So you're *The Example*.

SARAH. Again, these labels follow one around...

GLORIA. We're in trouble...

SARAH. And you're in turmoil?

GLORIA. Yes.

SARAH. It's why I'm here.

That's my signal.

> (*A beat.*)

Tell me.

GLORIA. Right, wow.

Well, I don't know where to start.

> (*A beat.*)

Okay, so he left his job because of a pigeon.

(*Brief silence. As* **SARAH** *expects more.*)

SARAH. Is that it?

GLORIA. Yes, I know it sounds ridiculous.
   All because of a bird.

SARAH. No, I meant. Is that it?
   That he left his job.
   That's all you're worried about.

GLORIA. It goes further back than that,
   but that's what happened today.
   I'm scared of what's about to happen from here.

SARAH. You mean as in money...

GLORIA. That, but as in everything.
   I think he needs help.

SARAH. What kind of help?

GLORIA. Professional help.
   Psychiatric help.

SARAH. Oh, I see.

   (*Pause.*)

GLORIA. Well...?

SARAH. The help needs to come from you, Gloria.
   You're his wife.
   And God will help.
   That's really all you need.

GLORIA. Okay.

SARAH. Can you do that?

GLORIA. I think so.

SARAH. You must.
   That's what you signed up for.
   That's your duty.
   That's your calling.

GLORIA. I know.

SARAH. Anything else?

GLORIA. No.
   You're not really how I imagined.

SARAH. How so?

GLORIA. You're very to the point.

SARAH. To The Word.

GLORIA. I thought you would talk more...

SARAH. More what?

GLORIA. I don't know, more – well, kinda biblically.

SARAH. Are you saying this has been
anti-climactic for you?

GLORIA. No, not at all.

SARAH. I'm just in the gospels.
I didn't write them.
That was the men.
Inspired by God.

GLORIA. No, it's been –

SARAH. I can talk like that if you want?

GLORIA. No, I mean, I have a bible.
This has been helpful.

SARAH. Okay. Glad I could help.

(*A beat.*)

And the pigeon...

GLORIA. Yes.

SARAH. Imperfect men make mistakes and often fall short
of being ideal family heads. But do not belittle your
husband
or try to take over his headship.
A wife does well to remember that.
A quiet and mild spirit is of great value.

GLORIA. Do you believe that?

SARAH. Now? Of course.
You don't?

GLORIA. If it's God's view.

SARAH. It is.

GLORIA. You're perfect.

SARAH. Well yes, Abraham and I, I don't know.

We have our ups and downs but we make it work!

    (They laugh.)

I've been far from perfect.
But the path is perfect and it is righteous and
it will protect you. You will learn that.
I have made dear mistakes, poor choices...
and in the end, the price for following one's
desires...it is too much to pay, too much to bear.
I urge you, Gloria...however challenging,
do not succumb to temptation, do not break.

GLORIA. God is great.

SARAH. He is.

And listen, I know it sounds tough
being a woman. But He's hard on the men too.
Read your bible.

GLORIA. I will.

    (A beat.)

Thank you.

2. Honolulu and New York – December 1980

> (**HE** *and* **GLORIA** *are at opposite sides of the stage.*)

HE. Hi.

GLORIA. Hi, I love you.

HE. I know. I love you too.

GLORIA. Oh.

> (**GLORIA** *starts to cry.*)

HE. Are the police with you?

GLORIA. No! The first call I got was a reporter.
Well, he didn't call me directly.
But the phone company called me.

HE. Are you at home?

GLORIA. Yeah. Your mom's here and Jean is gonna stay –

HE. Okay. Well I don't want to talk to anybody else.

GLORIA. I know.

HE. But I don't want you crying 'cause they can hear me.

GLORIA. Okay.

HE. Why aren't the police there? Call. Get the police over there.

GLORIA. Just what would – would I tell them?

HE. Just that you want them to come over.
To keep the press off of you.
Are they knocking on the door?

GLORIA. No. No one is.

HE. Well, they're gonna do that
and I want to protect you from that.

GLORIA. Yeah, but you don't want me to go there then?

HE. Go where?

GLORIA. To New York.

HE. No, no, no.
You just stay where you are.

GLORIA. Okay.

    (A beat.)

Has it hit you yet – what you've really done?

HE. I'm gonna have to go.

GLORIA. I love you. I always will love you.

HE. I know and I love you too and I need your love, and I, everything will be all right. You'll see.

GLORIA. What do I tell people?

HE. You don't talk at all.

GLORIA. Okay.

HE. You don't tell nobody nothin'.
It's not your position to do that.
You just trust me.
Don't talk.
Especially the press.
Don't let them bug you.

GLORIA. I won't talk. I won't go out at all.

HE. Did they give my name out and everything?

GLORIA. No, it's not on the news.
All they're saying is it's someone crazy in New York.
They don't even say.

HE. All right, don't talk about it.

GLORIA. Okay.

HE. I love you and I'll talk to you again and don't worry about anything, okay? Don't let them bother you.

GLORIA. Okay.

HE. You were my, you were my first concern.

GLORIA. I know.

HE. I'm just worried. You ought to call the police.
You know, you know, you'd like to know what to do.
And that you want somebody to come over, you know, a doctor and lawyer and whatever. Don't worry about the money.
You know that lawyer that we used, what's his name?

GLORIA. Um, I don't know, but I'll figure it out.

HE. Okay, I love you.

GLORIA. I love you, darling. I really do.

HE. See you. Love you.

3. New York – December 1980

(A diner. **HE** *moves to the bar where* **JUDE** *is sitting.)*

HE. Are you waiting for someone?

JUDE. As a matter of fact I was waiting for you.

HE. *(Encouraged.)* No kidding.

JUDE. What a letdown.

> *(***HE*** seems a little hurt.)*

I'm joking.

HE. Oh, right...

JUDE. I'm sorry. I *was* just teasing.

> *(A beat.)*

I'm Jude.

HE. Hey Jude. Don't be afraid, you were made –

JUDE. Stop it now.

> *(***JUDE*** groans. ***HE*** chuckles.)*

HE. I'm pretty original.

JUDE. Bonus points for getting a little deeper into the song. I normally just get, "Hey Jude, don't make it bad." Awful.

> *(***HE*** gestures to sit at the stool next to her.)*

HE. May I?

JUDE. What's your name?

HE. Holden.

JUDE. Stranger in town by the sounds of it. Where are you from?

HE. Hawaii. Honolulu. That's where I live. Decatur, Georgia originally. I'm just in the city for a few days.

JUDE. How do you like it so far?

HE. I heard John Lennon lives across the street.

JUDE. Yes, he does.

HE. I was hoping to meet him.

JUDE. I don't know if he's home right now, but rest assured, John Lennon is somewhere in New York City.

>   *(A beat.)*

I saw him earlier.

HE. That's so great.

JUDE. So you mean you came all this way to see John? That's committed.

HE. Well, yeah. I came here to see him.
But I'm pretty certain I'll be doing a lot more
while I'm here than just meeting John Lennon.

JUDE. There's lots to do.

HE. Hey, you ordered?

>   **(JUDE** *shakes her head.)*

Can I join you?

JUDE. Sure.

>   **(HE** *takes the stool next to* **JUDE.***)*

HE. I can't believe we're sitting right across from the building
where John Lennon lives. I mean, wow. You know?
Outside is the very sidewalk he walked, heck, John Lennon
may have even sat on this stool!

JUDE. *(Amused by his enthusiasm.)* Me and my friend Jeryl are considered family to the Lennons.

HE. You're putting me on.

JUDE. No, John and Yoko know us by name.
They stop and talk to us when they go for walks.
John likes to stroll through Central Park.
Every other afternoon, you know.
Like late afternoon.

HE. Is that right? Central Park, huh?

JUDE. Yeah.

HE. Do you know what happens to the ducks in the winter?

JUDE. No,what,why? What a random question!
You're silly.

HE. No, I'm being serious.
When the lake freezes over, where do the ducks go?

JUDE. *(Laughing.)* Cut it out!

HE. They must go somewhere! Where do they go!

JUDE. You're a nut. Jeryl and I met outside Dakota
and have been friends ever since. Whenever we go and
see a
movie or go for lunch we meet outside of there.
We've even been asked to run an errand for Lauren
Bacall.

HE. Wow! So there's a lot of famous people
who live here then? At the Dakota.

JUDE. Leonard Bernstein lives here as well.
You know, who Leonard Bernstein is?

HE. Yeah, I know who Leonard Bernstein is!
Wow, I never realized. Lauren Bacall.

> *(Pause.* **HE** *gestures to the television above
> and in the direction they are both facing.)*

How do you like our new president?

JUDE. Reagan? I think he's going to divide our country.

> *(A beat.)*

You don't?

HE. I don't know. But I think he's kind of a phony.

JUDE. *(Intrigued.)* How so?

> *(A slightly awkward silence.)*

HE. Look, I don't know. They just all seem a little phony,
you know?

> *(A beat.)*

I guess I don't follow politics real close.

JUDE. *(Mildly disappointed.)* Oh. Right.

HE. But I'm an avid reader. I really am.
I wish I'd bought one of John's books for him
to sign.

JUDE. You should pick up *Double Fantasy*.

HE. That's the new album, right?
You think?

JUDE. Sure, get it signed. Even if you don't, it's a great album anyway.
John and Yoko are amazing on it.

HE. That's a great idea. Yeah, maybe I'll do that.
Back in Hawaii they'd never believe I could get
John's autograph on his album.

JUDE. It'll be a great thing to show off.

HE. It really will. I'm a Beatle addict. I really am.
The music of the Beatles will one day be known, be ranked
alongside the great musical geniuses like Chopin, Beethoven, Bach
and Mozart. All those classics. Guaranteed.

JUDE. Hey, I can give you the names and phone numbers of other fans in City. They'd love to meet someone who came all this way. Here.

> *(She scribbles on a napkin.* **HE** *watches her as she writes.* **JUDE** *hands the napkin to* **HE**, *who absentmindedly wads the napkin and stuffs it in his pocket.)*

HE. Order anything you want my treat.

JUDE. No, really, you don't have to.

HE. Really. I'm buying. My treat.

> **(HE** *beckons for service.* **HONOLULU GUN STORE** *enters. He has all kinds of weaponry and ammunition attached to him.* **JUDE** *does not acknowledge any of the following.)*

HONOLULU GUN STORE. Can I help?

HE. I need something for protection.

You see, I've just been hearing noises and it's got me thinking.

I want to be ready.

HONOLULU GUN STORE. Sure. Okay.

Anything in mind?

HE. What would you recommend?

HONOLULU GUN STORE. Well, if you get a .22 and you have an intruder,

he's just gonna think you're Coco the Clown.

Cute little gun, it's fast, but don't do much damage.

But if you get a .38, nobody's gonna laugh at you.

A first-rate firearm. Smith and Wesson. Blue steel, snub nose,

it's solid, otherwise the same as a police service revolver.

Go on, hold it.

(**HONOLULU GUN STORE** *hands* **HE** *the .38.*)

HE. It feels nice.

HONOLULU GUN STORE. That will stop anything that gets in your way and it's flexible,

lightweight, reliable. It'll feel practically part of you.

Like a frickin' appendage.

You know some of these guns are like kids' toys,

but a Smith and Wesson, you can still crack somebody's skull

with it and it'll still come back dead on.

Are you interested in an automatic?

HE. How much for this?

(**HE** *hands back the .38.*)

HONOLULU GUN STORE. With specialized grips, 169 dollars.

HE. I'll take it.

HONOLULU GUN STORE. You won't regret it.

HE. Is that it? Do you need anything else?

HONOLULU GUN STORE. No, that's it pretty much.

(**HONOLULU GUN STORE** *exits. A beat.*)

HE. How was your omelet?

JUDE. Great. I always get that when I'm here.
How was your burger?

HE. Not cooked as well as I'd like.
And your coffee?

JUDE. Coffee is always good. The beer?

HE. Beer is always good.

(**HE** *grins.* **JUDE** *smiles back. A brief silence.*)

Something is going to be happening soon.
You're going to hear about me.

JUDE. You're gonna be famous or something?

HE. I just want you to be aware that something is going
to happen.

(*Brief silence.*)

JUDE. I'll keep a lookout.

(*A beat.*)

You know, I should really go.

HE. You're not leaving now are you?
We haven't seen John together, yet.
We're sure to see him soon.
I got a feeling about it.

JUDE. I don't think so. It's getting late and...
I don't think so. I've got to go.

HE. No!

(*A beat.*)

I mean, wait.
We're just getting to know each other.
How about hanging out some more, huh?
We can see a movie or a show or something...
and then grab dinner later. Seriously, my treat.

JUDE. Thanks, but I should go.
   Thank you for lunch.

HE. Hey, just a little while longer.

JUDE. I have to go. Good luck with John.
   The Lennons are great.
   They're great people.

4. Honolulu – May 1980

> (**HE** *is looking at a book intently.* **GLORIA** *enters.*)

GLORIA. Hey baby. Another book?

> (*No response.*)

How are those job applications?
You find anything?

> (*No response.*)

You know, Heather says it's a good time to get something.
She says they're hiring at a bunch of places.

> (*No response.*)

Have you had a good day?

HE. (*Without looking up.*) Did you see the bicycle?
I bought you a bicycle.
As a gift. It's downstairs.

GLORIA. That's for me?

> (*No response.*)

It's shiny. How much?

HE. Hey, come look at this book I got.

> (*He hands the book open on a page to* **GLORIA.**
> *She looks at the cover, then starts reading.*)

GLORIA. *John Lennon: One Day at a Time.*
I just started the book you gave me at lunchtime.
The one with Holden Cowfield. *Catcher in the* –

HE. *THE Catcher in the Rye.* And it's Caulfield.
Not cow field. Holden Caulfield.

> (*A beat.*)

No. I'm not saying read it.
The pictures. Look at the pictures.

GLORIA. Woah. He looks kinda old, huh?

I think Paul has aged the best.

Where's this?

HE. New York. He lives in New York City.

GLORIA. His apartment is NICE. Wow.

> (**GLORIA** *hands the book back to* **HE** *and sidles up to him. She starts to kiss his neck.* **HE** *is more concerned with the book.*)

Maybe we can get a place like that one day.

HE. *(Resentfully.)* Yeah, right.

> (**GLORIA** *continues to kiss* **HE***'s neck,* **HE** *tries to avoid her.*)

GLORIA. When we have our family...

HE. Hey, cut it out.

> (**GLORIA** *continues to kiss* **HE***'s neck.*)

GLORIA. You know, I know money could be better, but maybe this

is what we need, we said we wanted this someday

and now's a good time for me.

> (**GLORIA** *continues to kiss* **HE***'s neck.*)

HE. I said knock it off. Jeez.

> (**HE** *moves away from* **GLORIA**.)

Look at that, the decadent bastard.

GLORIA. Oh, what's decadent? He's rich.

He's rich because he's talented.

What's decadent?

HE. He's a fucking liar.

GLORIA. *A liar?* What are you even – what are you talking about?

What made you pick this up?

HE. Imagine no possessions, what do you call that?

Opulent apartment. Millions of dollars and yachts and cars

and country estates, laughing at people like us.

GLORIA. Nobody is laughing at us.

>   *(Silence.)*

You got me a bicycle?

HE. Yeah. To ride. You can ride to work on a bicycle.

GLORIA. Was it expensive?

HE. No, it's a bicycle. It cost what a bicycle costs.
We sold the car, I don't want you taking the bus anymore,
I bought you a bicycle. Does it not make you crazy?
Looking at that? The phony bastard.

GLORIA. Oh, you are always using that word.

>   *(A beat.)*

I love The Beatles. I have their records.
I like John Lennon. A phony.
Why do you use that word so much?

HE. Because my world's crawling with them.
I have to look at things like this every doggone day!

GLORIA. Have you eaten? I'm kinda hungry.

>   *(No response.)*

>   *(Firmly.)* Have you eaten?
I'm kinda hungry.

HE. No, not hungry.

GLORIA. I'm going to make myself something.

>   *(A beat.)*

Thank you for the bicycle. It's very sweet.

HE. *(After a beat.)* Yeah.

>   *(**SARAH** enters urgently.)*

GLORIA. Now do you see? John Lennon now?
I mean, really? I can't live like this.

SARAH. Yes, you can.

GLORIA. *(Firmly.)* No. I can't.

>   *(**ROBERT** enters.)*

ROBERT.

It was a soul-searching
drive over here I have to
say.

HE.

You know, do you?

ROBERT.

Sir, I... I just sense...

GLORIA.

I can't do this. Not on my
own.

SARAH.

You're not on your own.

HE.

First, a review from the
last meeting.

ROBERT.

Very well. The sales of
the Rockwell and the
Dali went through. You
decided not to pay back
your father-in-law and
you sold the car, so the
economy is a little more
stable. Gloria on the
other hand –

HE.

I don't need to talk about
her.

ROBERT.

With respect, sir, that
was what the remainder
of our last meeting was
about.

HE.

So we're done?

ROBERT.

Unless we discuss Gloria.

HE.

(Snaps.) Did you not hear me? I said I didn't want to!

ROBERT.

Well, then. That's all I have.

GLORIA.

I should call his mom.

SARAH.

That will only upset him more.

GLORIA.

I should call someone. A hospital or something.

SARAH.

(A little sharply.) And tell them *what* exactly?

(A beat.)

GLORIA.

I need to fix my husband.

SARAH.

You need to guide your husband towards the Lord.

HE.

I've become concerned about my personal safety. My protection.

I want to buy a handgun.

ROBERT.

Yes, sir.

HE.

Most likely a .38 caliber, I
figure I need between one
and two hundred dollars
for such an item

(No response.)

You disapprove?

ROBERT.

The funds are yours, sir,
but –

HE.

Good. I would also need
around five hundred
dollars for a trip to New
York City.

ROBERT.

New York City. Five
hundred dollars.

HE.

I also need between
fifteen hundred and two
thousand for hotels,
entertainment and
expenses, uh...just in
case.

ROBERT.

This is some outlay.

GLORIA.

Maybe it's me.

Maybe I make him like
this.

Maybe he'd be better
without me.

SARAH.

You're not listening to me.

GLORIA.

There isn't time! He is sick!

I have to do something.

SARAH.

We are never more like Satan, when we

do our own thing.

GLORIA.

What? He needs to change.

Or I need to leave!

SARAH.

Satan said, "I will be like God."

You're saying you want to play God.

GLORIA.

He is sick! Can't you understand that?

Can't you see that?

HE.

I'd like you to inform defense that I need such an amount for an emergency operation to be implemented within the next week.

(A beat.)

What?

ROBERT.

I'm sure the senate would be grateful to learn more

                              details of this emergency
                              operation, given the
                              figures requested.

                         HE.

                              It's just because I've
                              decided
                              to make a stand and be
                              somebody. Because I
                              cannot continue being
                              a nobody. Because I
                              am rotting away on the
                              inside. Because I'm dying.

                         ROBERT.

                              Dying, sir? How can this
                              be?

SARAH.

Be gentle. Submit to him.
Speak with humility and
respect.
That's how you win him
over.

                         HE.

                              This quest and my
                              identity lie in New York
                              City and that is where I
                              must go.

                         ROBERT.

                              Why New York?

                         HE.

                              Somebody from my
                              childhood, a hero to me,
                              someone you may know,
                              has betrayed me

                         ROBERT.

                              Who?

SARAH.

He will want to see what
it is that makes such a
difference in your life and
he will follow.

GLORIA.

He introduced me to
Christianity.

SARAH.

I know he did.
But he's stepped off the
path.
But he will return.

                                    HE.

I cite this book as my
evidence. John Lennon
living in an opulent
New York apartment
overlooking Central Park.
I didn't even know he
lived in New York, but
he's been there for years.
I assumed he was in
England, in a castle or
something like that. But
no, he's there in New York
City. All that stuff he said
he stood for...all phony.
He's just a rich bastard
like all the other phony
rich bastards that run the
world.

GLORIA.

Are you real? I mean, as
you stand
before me now?

SARAH.

(Offended slightly.) Well, what do you think?

GLORIA.

I hope you are.

I'm afraid.

SARAH.

I know.

GLORIA.

I love him, but lately...he scares me.

I'm scared of what he may do to himself.

SARAH.

Do not give way to fear. Don't be afraid.

Continue to pray for your husband.

God will work things out for the good

and His glory.

HE.

He's a fraud. The whole thing was just a scam, just one big hoax. I was inspired with false idealism. These ideals, these beliefs, I've lived by them, I've carried them around with me all my life. I believed it all, but here he admits he was just saying that stuff.

That it was baloney. Just publicity stunts that

didn't mean anything. I worshipped him, but it was just one big trick, and I fell for it, I fell for all of it and it's crippled me, he's made my life a joke. I have great confirmation and he has to be stopped. Let me be clear, he has had a lot to do with how I've turned out, and probably how a lot of others just like me have turned out. This betrayal has to be punished. I've decided that I must kill John Lennon. I've given this a lot of thought. But it will be a very difficult mission and I need your assistance.

SARAH.

And hospitals, doctors, professionals...

GLORIA.

Yes?

SARAH.

(Ominously.) Be careful who you talk to about this.

(A beat.)

SARAH.

Do you promise?

GLORIA.

Yes.

SARAH.

Don't get in God's way.

>   *(A beat.)*

The world doesn't understand, Gloria.

But you are not living for the world,

you are in God's Holy Nation.

You have been chosen to magnify him.

GLORIA.

I will.

>   **ROBERT.**
>
>   I can say the consensus will be that this is an absurd idea. Wholly unproductive –
>
>   **HE.**
>
>   Robert.
>
>   **ROBERT.**
>
>   A very non-productive decision that you have made.
>
>   **HE.**
>
>   Robert!
>
>   **ROBERT.**
>
>   If you embark on this crusade, you will cause a great deal of harm and absolute mayhem. It will cause pain and grief not only to yourself, but for very, very many people.
>
>   For God's sake, man,

think of the people in your life. Think of your mother. Think of Gloria. Think of yourself.

HE.

I've thought of myself. I've thought of my mom and I've thought of my wife. I've also thought of my pathetic father and all my phony friends.

Without your help –

ROBERT.

We can't help you with this.

HE.

Without your help –

ROBERT.

We cannot go along with this. It's outrageous.

HE.

Very well. I respect your decision. I want to thank you for all your service in the past.

ROBERT.

Are you firing me?

SARAH. Gloria, submission is beautiful not wrong.

Be pure, and be reverent.

They will not be won over by the force of your arguments,

but by your kindness.

The blessings are won without words.

(**SARAH** *gestures to* **GLORIA** *to go over to* **HE.** *She does.*)

SARAH. God saved you so you can glorify Him.
So you can highlight Him, to show Him off.
So you must obey Him.

GLORIA. I will.

(To **HE.***)* Are you sure I can't make you a sandwich?

HE. No, I'm good. Thanks.

GLORIA. Okay. Just tell me when.

> *(**GLORIA** kisses **HE** and exits. **HE** and **ROBERT** stare at each other. **HE** then exits abruptly, leaving **ROBERT** and **SARAH** alone onstage. Silence as **SARAH** glares at **ROBERT**. **ROBERT** puckishly, magician-like, produces a lei from his sleeve. **ROBERT** gestures to **SARAH** to have him put it on her. She is unimpressed.)*

ROBERT. *(Laughs briefly, puts the lei around his neck.)* Very well.

SARAH. For one so fallen, you're sure of yourself,
I'll give you that.

ROBERT. If it's a compliment, I'll take it.
You're looking good, Sarah.
A little tightly-wound perhaps,
but nevertheless...

> *(A beat.)*

How's Abraham?

SARAH. Abraham is fine.

ROBERT. Domestic bliss.
Send my best, won't you?
And Isaac?
How's little Isaac?

SARAH. Isaac is not so little.

ROBERT. Does he take after his dad?

> *(Silence.)*

They grow up so fast, don't they?
One minute they're that high,

and the next they're even taller.

You have the whole package.

Dark family secrets not withstanding

of course. You don't have to thank me.

It was an honor to serve.

SARAH. *(Ignoring last remark.)* And you? British now, it seems.

ROBERT. *(Preening a little.)* You're impressed? What the customer wants,

the customer gets.

As well you know.

Think it was something conjured from his childhood,

but who am I to judge?

It works. I'm growing rather fond of it.

SARAH. What do you want?

ROBERT. What do I want?

SARAH. Yes.

ROBERT. With Mark?

SARAH. Yes.

ROBERT. If you remember, it doesn't really work like that.

It was he who called for me.

He needs my help.

He needs to find himself.

Who doesn't? It's a need within us.

    (A beat.)

And you?

What about *you*?

What does Sarah *want* these days?

SARAH. Gloria is in turmoil.

ROBERT. Turmoil? Sounds precarious.

And here you are to protect her,

to save the day.

To "fix it," as it were.

SARAH. To keep her on the right path.

ROBERT. Your path?

SARAH. God's path.

ROBERT. Oh God's path. He has a reformed little helper.
How splendid.

> *(A beat.)*

Sarah, Sarah, burden bearer.

Poster child of the co-dependent.

SARAH. I'm warning you.

ROBERT. Warning me of what?

Tell me, do you need to be loved or love to be needed?

SARAH. WHAT ARE YOU DOING HERE?

ROBERT. HE ASKED ME HERE!

> *(A beat.)*

Gosh look at that, I too can raise my voice.

But let's not make a hullabaloo, for old times' sake.

SARAH. They are building a life together here.

ROBERT. They are dying here. *Life together.*

They're anaemic! But he has desire, I like that.

He's got fire in his belly. It's intestinal with him.

He wants to be somebody and wants it NOW!

He needs to do his thing, she hers, and you should mind
your own beeswax. She can walk for all I care.

But neither can be boxed in like a couple of battery
hens.

It's no life, is it? Suffocated. Constipated.

Practically dead. Like you.

SARAH. That's hogwash. That's not even... That's not.

You have absolutely no idea what you're talking about.

ROBERT. *Hogwash?*

> *(A beat.)*

I mean, what even happened to you?

You used to be so full of life.

Of instinct.

Of desire.

Of fire!

You used to be alive.

You used to be human.

Now what? You're a notion, a mere idea.

An Example? A Mirage.

I'm not even sure you even exist, if you want to know the truth.

What do you think about that?

SARAH. I exist.

ROBERT. Prove it.

SARAH. What?

>   *(A beat.)*

ROBERT. Prove it. Let me take a closer look at you.

SARAH. No! You, you beast!

ROBERT. Prove it. Come here.

Let me touch you.

SARAH. Absolutely not.

ROBERT. Afraid I won't feel anything or

afraid you might like it?

>   *(Silence.)*

SARAH. All these tricks and games, you have.

ROBERT. No trick. No game. Just prove it.

>   *(A beat.)*

Come here.

>   (**SARAH** *hesitates for a moment and then goes to* **ROBERT** *to where they are face-to-face.*)

Take my hand.

SARAH. No.

ROBERT. Fine.

>   *(Pause.)*

Take my hand.

We've done a lot worse together once upon a time.

> *(A beat.)*

You can hold my hand for a moment, can't you?

> *(Pause, then **SARAH** gives **ROBERT** her hand.)*

There. Don't be nervous.
That's not so bad, is it?
Your hands are sweaty.

SARAH. I'm sorry.

ROBERT. Don't apologize. I rather like it.
You're trembling a little...

> *(**ROBERT** pulls her in slightly and smells her.)*

You smell amazing.

> *(A beat.)*

SARAH. Thank you.

> *(**ROBERT** moves behind her, never letting go of her hand.)*

ROBERT. I stand corrected. It really is you.

> *(A beat.)*

SARAH. It's me.

ROBERT. I've missed you, Sarah.

> *(A beat.)*

Have you missed me?

> *(**ROBERT** starts to kiss her neck, **SARAH** pulls away.)*

(Laughs.) Gah! Almost!
Almost!

> *(Silence.)*

So close. Well done.
You're made of stronger stuff now.
I'll give you that.

> *(A brief silence.)*

SARAH. Don't flatter yourself.

It doesn't take so much strength to resist
where you're concerned.

I actually pity you.

ROBERT. Really.

SARAH. A woman needs a man, a real man, and you,
well look at you. You sneer at others but who are you?
A boy. A child. A mirage? You're the mirage.

You prey on weakness because anything else would
be punching above your weight. Your achievements are mediocre,

yet you inflate them to the sky. You destroy things because you simply
don't have the imagination to create anything.

You hate that, don't you?

You're envious, jealous.

You're completely expendable and you know that too,
but you keep coming back.

It's needy. You're needy.

It's not an attractive trait.

> *(A beat.)*

This ends right now.

ROBERT. *Ends right now?* It's just the beginning.

The cat's out of the bag. The train has left the station.
The bull is out of the gate!

You're too late. It's been...well, willed.

You can understand that now, can't you?

> *(A beat.)*

And... *Don't have the imagination to create anything?*
Now, you know that's not true.

Give Isaac a hug, won't you?

From his old man.

5. New York – December 1980

HE. I'm at the Sheraton...

That's right... Room 2730...

Yes... Do you have any exotic women?

I would prefer a woman who isn't American...

That's nice. But there's one condition: She doesn't talk.

She's got to be quiet... I don't want someone who will talk.

If she's quiet, I will tip very well...

Thank you.

> *(Lights up as* **SUNNY** *enters. She has an Eastern European accent. She wears a green dress.)*

SUNNY. Mr. Caulfield?

HE. Yes. Uh, Holden.

Thank you for being here.

> *(***SUNNY*** *smiles.)*

SUNNY. You should thank the agency.

> *(Silence.)*

HE. I'm not perverted. I'm clean. I'm not a freak.

SUNNY. That is...nice.

HE. I'm not even all that interested in having sex, if you really want to know. I just wanted the companionship of a lady this evening.

I have a feeling tomorrow will be an extremely challenging day for me.

SUNNY. Are you here on business? For a conference?

HE. Business, yeah. I can order a round of drinks from room service.

They're really great here. Great service.

I always stay at the Sheraton when I'm in New York.

We'll get them in next to no time.

We really will.

SUNNY. I do not drink. I am sorry.

HE. Not to worry. There is no need for apologies.

I didn't intend to use you for myself.

This is your night off.

We'll do whatever you want to do.

SUNNY. I do not know what I want to do.

HE. Well, why don't you take your dress off and come and join me here.

SUNNY. I can do that for you.

HE. Not for me.

For you.

Just wait and see.

(**SUNNY** *pulls her dress over her head and holds it at arm's length.*)

SUNNY. Is there a place I can hang up my dress?

It has just been cleaned.

HE. Brand clean?

SUNNY. Yes.

(**HE** *takes the dress from* **SUNNY** *and hangs the dress up.* **HE** *returns to her.* **ROBERT** *enters and hangs back, watching them both.*)

HE. You're wonderful. You know that? I'd like to give you a massage.

SUNNY. Can we turn on the radio?

HE. Uh...sure. Any reason?

SUNNY. I think another guest at the hotel saw me arrive in your room.

I do not want to go to jail.

(**HE** *raises his hand. A jaunty Christmas song plays on the radio.**)

---

*A license to produce *Two of Us* does not include a performance license for any third-party or copyrighted music. Licensees should create an original composition or use music in the public domain. For further information, please see Music Use Note on page 3.

HE. Just relax...

> (**HE** *begins to massage* **SUNNY**'s *shoulders*.)

ROBERT. Oh sir, this isn't you is it... SIR?!
Still mad at me, eh? You know, I never left you.
All the others did but I've stayed around.
With you.

> (*No response.*)

We should go home, eh? Back to Gloria.
What about it? Back to the wife. THE WIFE!
...No, not even a twitch.

> (**SUNNY** *gives a moan of pleasure.*)

HE. How does this feel?

SUNNY. Good.

HE. Just good?

SUNNY. Very good.

ROBERT. Sir? Uh, sir?

HE. Go away.

> (*Leans into* **SUNNY**.)

A real man doesn't have to take from a woman.
He can give.

> (**HE** *starts to kiss* **SUNNY**'s *neck.*)

6. Honolulu - December 1980

(**HUSBAND** *and* **GLORIA** *are holding hands during prayer.*)

HUSBAND. ...And we still praise our Father God for the gracious gifts

and severe mercies. For all these things, and your love for us,

we thank you in your son Lord Jesus's name.

Amen.

GLORIA. Amen.

HUSBAND. I'm sorry we can't help you, Gloria.

I certainly would if I could. You know that, right?

GLORIA. Of course, and I hate to ask.

He would be very angry with me if he knew I asked you.

HUSBAND. But he's not here.

He's in New York.

GLORIA. Right.

HUSBAND. Running up the credit card.

GLORIA. Yes.

HUSBAND. You did the right thing.

Even if we can be of absolutely no help to you.

GLORIA. Money's not everything. I value our friendship.

Your family has always been good to me.

HUSBAND. Tell me more about this book.

What's in it that has gripped him and led him so astray?

GLORIA. Well, I don't know... I...

It's about a teenager.

HUSBAND. And he's the catcher?

GLORIA. I guess so.

Or he wants to do that.

HUSBAND. What? What's he catching?

GLORIA. Uh...children, I guess. Innocent children.
Who are playing in the Rye. But they're in danger...
or something. Because they're going to fall off the cliff,
if they're not careful. Or if someone doesn't protect
them.
That's what this teenager boy wants to do with his life.

HUSBAND. How curious.
And is there blasphemy?

GLORIA. Yes. Sometimes. Well, most of the time actually.
He seems to hate everything. Holden.
That's the character's name. Phoniness, really.
Holden hates phonies. Holden says it a lot.
And my husband does. To him, everything is phony
now.
I don't know, it's like he hates everything too.

HUSBAND. Colossians 3:8. "Rid yourself of anger, rage,
malice, slander
and filthy language"...

GLORIA. It's as if he...

HUSBAND. What?

GLORIA. It's as if he...he's not the man I fell in love with.
He was always so compassionate. Unbelievably so.
I was in awe of him. The stories he would tell about the
children
he met in Vietnam, in Nepal when he went away,
around the world, just before we started dating,
the way he introduced me to Jesus Christ and the way
he would talk about God. He spoke as if he was filled
with the Holy Spirit,
and I believe he was. I don't see any of that now.

HUSBAND. You can guide him, Gloria. Never give up on
that.
Never give up on your efforts to guide your husband.

(**WIFE** *enters cheerfully.*)

WIFE. And the dishes are done!

GLORIA. You really didn't have to do that.
Thank you.

> (**WIFE** *very naturally sits on* **HUSBAND***'s lap.*
> **HUSBAND** *kisses* **WIFE**.)

HUSBAND. Nice job, honey.

> (*A beat.*)

So this is why you think he's gone to New York?

GLORIA. I don't know. He said he wanted to start writing a children's book.
That's why he's gone there.

WIFE. He's gone to New York to write a children's book?
What about his job?

HUSBAND. He quit apparently.

WIFE. He's walked out on *another* job? Oh honey.
He wasn't even there a month, right?

GLORIA. He said he doesn't want to be a security guard.

HUSBAND. It's all very curious. Well, if you'll both excuse me,
I need to use the restroom.

WIFE. Oh, I need to go.

HUSBAND. Oh, well you go.

WIFE. No, you go.

HUSBAND. Okay.

> (**HUSBAND** *and* **WIFE** *both laugh and kiss once
> more.* **HUSBAND** *exits. Silence.*)

GLORIA. I love him. More than anything.
I just don't know whether I can...

WIFE. Whether you can what, honey?

GLORIA. Whether I can save him.

WIFE. (*Encouragingly.*) Only God can save him, Gloria.
God will be the one who will change your husband.

GLORIA. (*After a beat.*) Are you happy?

WIFE. (*Surprised, laughs.*) How do you mean?

Whatever made you ask that?

What a strange question!

GLORIA. I'm sorry, I...

forget I asked that...

> *(Silence.* **WIFE***'s pleasant demeanor drops somewhat.)*

WIFE. Wait, did he tell you?

GLORIA. About what? ...Oh, only a little...

> *(Silence.)*

WIFE. That we may lose the house?

GLORIA. Yes.

I'm sorry.

While you were in the kitchen.

I'm sorry.

WIFE. Well...no matter what the outcome,

we know that God's plan is perfect.

GLORIA. You knew it wouldn't work, didn't you?

You told me at the time.

WIFE. I didn't.

GLORIA. You did. You knew it was a bad investment.

You said –

WIFE. I never said that.

GLORIA. You said it was a crazy risk and that you had two

young children –

WIFE. *(Snapping a little.)* Are we going to talk about your husband gallivanting around

New York or my husband that is right down the hallway, Gloria?

GLORIA. I'm sorry. I didn't mean to –

WIFE. I have a *profound respect* for my husband,

as you should have for yours.

I mean, gosh, how would he feel if he could

hear you this evening?

No wonder he feels isolated.

Hearing you complain about him in such a way with your

mutual friends at a party, and to *my* husband.

GLORIA. I am not complaining.

WIFE. You are.

GLORIA. I have no one I can talk to about this!

> *(Silence.)*

I apologize.

> *(A beat.)*

WIFE. He shouldn't have told you that.

We are working it out.

GLORIA. I didn't mean to embarrass you.

I asked for a small loan.

That's why he told me.

WIFE. You asked my husband for a loan?

GLORIA. We're desperate.

WIFE. Does your husband know you're doing this?

GLORIA. No.

WIFE. I see.

> *(Pause.)*

He shouldn't have told you that. We are working it out.

GLORIA. I'm sorry.

I just am beginning to question...this way...

this submitting to –

WIFE. Gloria, I do not like this conversation and I do not like where this is headed.

> *(An awkward silence.)*

GLORIA. I had to do something. I don't think he's – he's sick, we're broke,

we need to survive. I don't even know who I am anymore.

And I can't just hope things get better!

WIFE. We are all sinners, Gloria, Christ died for us. You have been

bought by the precious blood of Jesus Christ.

Or has that changed now things are a little difficult?

GLORIA. No.

WIFE. This is not tarot cards or Emperor worship or Shinto or...

or Buddhism or wherever it is you came from.

GLORIA. Woah, wherever it is I came from? I'm *American*!

WIFE. Oh now you're being preposterous.

I did not mean it like that.

GLORIA. What did you mean?

WIFE. You are Christian now. You are a wife now.

It's not just an accessory or something you can just *try on* like...

a sweater from JCPenney, or some pair of shoes. If you want hope for your home and your husband,

you must go back to the cross. You must go back

to the Lord Jesus Christ, who offers Himself to you

and offered his life. As Jesus submitted to God the Father,

so too must we, following His example, be submissive to our

husbands. *That* is the teaching. And yes, since you mention it,

that's also American.

> *(A beat.)*

GLORIA. You're right.

WIFE. Obedience to God's work will bring blessings to your marriage.

> *(Silence.* **HUSBAND** *re-enters.)*

HUSBAND. You might want to give it five minutes in there, honey.

> (**WIFE** *glares at her* **HUSBAND**.)

Something about that potato salad.

WIFE. (*A little tersely.*) It'll be fine.

> (**WIFE** *exits.*)

HUSBAND. I lit a match.

> Is she okay?

GLORIA. I should probably go to bed.

HUSBAND. Are you sure?

> (*No response.*)

> You look upset.

> (*Silence.*)

> Oh my child...

> (**HUSBAND** *embraces and comforts* **GLORIA.**)

> There, there.

> Look, suffering will either make you bitter or better.

> It'll either drive you away from God or push you towards God.

> But it is up to you, how you react to hardships.

> And you can be the example to him through this.

GLORIA. I know.

HUSBAND. And for the love of Peter, when he's back from New York,

> tell him to burn that book, if it's making him crazy!

> Hey, was that a smile?

GLORIA. Thank you. You're very kind. Thank you.

HUSBAND. You're very special, Gloria. Very special.

> He needs to honor you, as Christ did with all women,

> and treat you correctly but he needs to be back here ASAP

> to do that. He cannot opt out of that. It's not an option.

> He cannot relinquish the family leadership

> and be considerate to you and bestow the honor you deserve,

> when he's out there watching The Rockettes.

It's being a husband. It's being a man.

When he returns, pray together.

Remember, you're a team.

GLORIA. Thank you.

> (**HUSBAND** *leans in and kisses* **GLORIA** *on the lips. When it's clear that this is not how friends kiss each other, she pushes him away.*)

You need to go. It's late.

HUSBAND. My word, it is. Let me give her a holler.

Tell her you're kicking us out.

GLORIA. No, really. I can –

HUSBAND. *(Gathering his* **WIFE***'s things.)* Don't worry.

HONEY?! GLORIA'S TIRED!!

(To **GLORIA***.)* She's usually pretty fast.

> *(They listen.)*

Here she comes.

So you're working tomorrow?

GLORIA. Yes.

> (**SARAH** *and* **WIFE** *enter and stand either side of* **HUSBAND***. The trio-in-a-line face* **GLORIA***, who is rendered speechless.)*

WIFE. It was so nice to see you, Gloria.

SARAH. Yes, interesting talk.

HUSBAND. You bet. Great party.

You know, you're welcome at our place anytime.

You know that, right? God bless.

> *(No response.)*

WIFE. Gloria?

> *(No response.)*

SARAH. Gloria?

GLORIA. Right. Good night.

7. Honolulu and New York – December 1980

> (**HE** *and* **GLORIA** *are at opposite sides of the stage.*)

GLORIA. Yes, I will accept the charges...hello?

HE. It's me.

GLORIA. Hi.

HE. I know I said I wasn't gonna call –

GLORIA. I'm glad you did.

HE. But I feel lonely.

GLORIA. What time is it there?

It must be –

HE. It's close to three a.m.

GLORIA. What are you doing?

HE. You sound like you're doing okay.

GLORIA. I am. I am okay.

I finally finished that book you gave me.

HE. Yeah. What'd you think?

GLORIA. There were some parts I wanted to read again.

HE. Yeah, but what did you think?

GLORIA. You were right. Holden Caulfield reminds me of you.

HE. You understand me better?

GLORIA. He's sixteen years old, right?

HE. Yeah.

> (*Pause.*)

But you understand me better?

GLORIA. I understand why you've started using the word "phony" so much.

HE. Be serious, Gloria.

> (*No response.*)

Well?

GLORIA. He's sensitive. And he has a good heart. Like you.

And he wants to protect people. Like you.
He also seems sad and angry. Like you.
Is that why you've gone to New York?

(Silence.)

Are you...are you being sensible with money?

HE. Don't tell me to come home.

GLORIA. I wasn't going to.

HE. I can hear that you were going to.

GLORIA. I wasn't.

(Pause.)

HE. How was the party?

(A beat.)

GLORIA. It was nice. We had a good time.

HE. Listen, I'm sorry I didn't wish you a happy party when I left. I just wasn't thinking about stuff like that. I'm sorry.

(Pause.)

GLORIA. Hey...

HE. Yeah?

GLORIA. Am I...what you want?
What you need, I mean?
Am I doing a good job?

HE. Gloria.

GLORIA. What?

(A silence.)

HE. How's Mom?

GLORIA. She's good.
What's the weather like?

HE. It's real nice.
Not cold or rainy like last time.
Just real nice.

GLORIA. Have you been to a show yet?

HE. No. Not yet. Listen, I love you very much.

More than anyone else.

And I know I do things which don't make it seem that I do,

but I really do. Love you.

And I always will.

GLORIA. I know. I –

HE. I want you to call Mom soon.

Maybe tomorrow and tell her that I love her.

I love her and that I'm glad she's feeling better.

(*A beat.*)

I hope I didn't wake you. I couldn't sleep.

GLORIA. You didn't. I was just reading my bible.

Do you have one there?

HE. Yeah. It's on my nightstand.

GLORIA. I think you should work on your problems one by one.

And maybe the first one is to get back with Christ again.

And then maybe He can help you with all your other ones.

Or maybe not. Maybe there's another way.

Maybe we can find another way. Together.

The two of us.

HE. You're right. Look, I'm sorry for calling collect.

I just realized when you answered that I could have just put it on my hotel bill.

GLORIA. I love you. I miss you.

HE. I love you and I miss you.

GLORIA. Bye.

8. New York – December 1980

*(Early evening. Dimly lit. **PHOTOGRAPHER**, dressed for a New York winter, fiddles with his expensive looking camera and equipment that is hung around his neck. **HE** enters excitedly. He wears an overcoat and a Russian looking fur hat. He carries a vinyl LP in his left hand. There is something of condescension toward **HE** from **PHOTOGRAPHER**.)*

HE. Gosh! That's pretty amazing.
Stars don't usually put the date on it, do they?
This is unique.

PHOTOGRAPHER. Yeah. Looks like you struck gold.

HE. It's a collector's item! Wow. Back in Hawaii,
they'll flip out if they knew I met John Lennon
and got his autograph!

PHOTOGRAPHER. It's certainly something.

*(**HE** holds the album close to his chest.)*

HE. Look, I'm sorry if I came on a little heavy before.
I've been standing out here for three days now.
I just got a little sore, I guess.

PHOTOGRAPHER. Right. Just calm down.

HE. I am calm. I just want to start over.

PHOTOGRAPHER. What the hell?
You start up a conversation with a guy like
he's your best friend, then you do a complete
one-eighty and get all hostile?

HE. I said I was sorry about that. I apologized.
What can I say? I'm a big dope and I'm bored and
I'm far away from home, so I try to talk to people for a bit of...
humanity. I'm tired, so I guess that's why I flew off the handle. I'm sorry. Okay?

PHOTOGRAPHER. Well, you got what you came for.

(**PHOTOGRAPHER** *notices* **HE**'s *holding of the album.* **PHOTOGRAPHER** *returns to his camera equipment.*)

And nobody's going to steal your album around here. Whatever it is you've heard about New York.

(*Silence.*)

HE. Hey, wait a minute! Hold on! Listen!
I'll give you anything for that picture!

PHOTOGRAPHER. What picture?

HE. Come on, I saw you snapping away, man.
I must have been in one of them. I'll give you anything. Anything. Wait a minute. Did I have my hat on or off when
you took it? I didn't want to be photographed standing beside
John Lennon in this stupid Russian hat. Was my hat on or off?
Do you remember?

PHOTOGRAPHER. I think you were wearing your hat.

HE. Damn it!

PHOTOGRAPHER. You look fine.

HE. Damn it!

PHOTOGRAPHER. (*Amused.*) You need a moment or somethin'?

HE. Okay. Okay. Listen, is there any way you can get that film processed tonight?

PHOTOGRAPHER. No chance.

HE. Is there any way I can get that picture tonight?

PHOTOGRAPHER. No chance, bud. I live in New Jersey.
I can't develop and print 'til tomorrow.

HE. I'll give you a hundred dollars for that picture tonight.

PHOTOGRAPHER. Are you not hearing me?
I can't develop and print 'til tomorrow.

HE. I will buy it off you. If you're here tomorrow.

PHOTOGRAPHER. I'm always here.

HE. I'll give you fifty dollars for that one picture.
Meet me here tomorrow and I'll give you fifty
dollars for that picture of me with John Lennon –
if it comes out alright. Is that a deal?

PHOTOGRAPHER. Tomorrow? Okay, sure.

HE. Wait 'til they see that photograph back in Honolulu.
Me standing next to John Lennon.

> (**PHOTOGRAPHER** *begins taking apart his
> camera and packing it away.*)

PHOTOGRAPHER. Yeah.

HE. What are you doing?

PHOTOGRAPHER. I gotta get back to North Arlington.
Get home. Get some sleep.

HE. No. Listen. I'm sorry about before.
I'm staying at the Sheraton. I don't know why
I got all defensive when you asked.

PHOTOGRAPHER. You've apologized. I'm cool.
But my day is done and I gotta go.
I'll be back here tomorrow.
I'll bring your picture.

HE. You really oughta stay a while longer.
They could come back any minute.

PHOTOGRAPHER. They'll have gone to the studio.
They're out for the night.

HE. I got a feeling they'll be back before midnight.

PHOTOGRAPHER. I'm not staying here 'til midnight.

HE. Or sooner. I just got a feeling.

PHOTOGRAPHER. You've got his autograph.
Mission accomplished, give it up and get some rest.
Sheraton's expensive. Stay there and relax.
Get your buck's worth.

HE. But suppose you don't see him again?

PHOTOGRAPHER. *(Exiting.)* I'll see him again, pal. Don't you
worry.

HE. Suppose you don't?

> (**PHOTOGRAPHER** *continues to exit. Now ignoring him.*)

(Desperately.) Suppose you don't see him again?

> (**HE** *begins pacing up and down, still clutching the album tightly against his chest.*)

9. New York – December 1980

(Around midnight. Darker. **HE** *anxiously paces back and forth to stave off the cold.* **ROBERT** *enters dressed as a little boy. He wears shorts and t-shirt and a Confederate hat. Around his waist is a toy gun holster with a toy gun in it. He now speaks with the same accent as* **HE**.*)*

HE. What are you doing here?

ROBERT. Any sign of him?

HE. What?

ROBERT. The foe.

Your nemesis.

HE. What are you wearing? You look ridiculous.

ROBERT. Says the guy wearing that hat.

> *(A beat.)*

You don't remember this?

HE. *(Considers for a moment.)* Vaguely.

ROBERT. This is what you used to wear, wasn't it?

Back in the day.

HE. Why are you talking like that?

I thought you were...

ROBERT. What?

HE. I don't know.

I thought you were British.

ROBERT. Not now. Just a good ol' American boy.

From Decatur, Georgia. Just like you.

> *(A beat.)*

Hey

FROM DECATUR TO THE DAKOTA...

HE. That's not a song.

ROBERT. I made it up. You don't like it?

HE. Just shut up, will ya?

(*Pause.*)

ROBERT. Can I see it?

HE. What?

ROBERT. What's in your pocket.

HE. No.

ROBERT. Come on.

HE. No.

ROBERT. Why?

HE. Someone may see.

ROBERT. Who? Just a peek.

Come on.

Open your pocket.

I just wanna take a quick look.

> (**ROBERT** *moves right up to* **HE. HE** *opens the pocket of his overcoat and* **ROBERT** *peers in.*)

Nice.

Personal protection?

> (**HE** *closes his pocket and* **ROBERT** *moves away from* **HE.**)

Your history and they allow you to get a gun.

God bless America

Got your album signed, I saw.

HE. You were watching?

ROBERT. I'm always watching.

HE. You said you wanted no part in this.

ROBERT. I was fulfilling my role as your Chief Adviser.

I had a responsibility.

Since you went solo and abandoned us,

I don't know what to

do with myself.

I've just been lounging around the house.

HE. You don't have a house.

And it was you who abandoned me.

ROBERT. Whatever. What can I say? I need a cause.

HE. That was you last night. In the hotel room?

ROBERT. Just donning the cap.

Old habits die hard, I guess.

It didn't stop you, did it?

You horn dog.

Hey, I didn't stay to watch that.

She was a looker alright, I'll give you that.

Was she worth the dough?

Had a little more shape to her than your

little Geisha back home.

HE. *(Snaps.)* Don't talk about Gloria that way.

ROBERT. O-kay. Easy. Sheesh, I'm sorry.

> *(Pause.* **ROBERT** *starts to whistle quietly.)*

HE. Look.

ROBERT. Yep?

HE. I just want you to leave. I don't need this.

I don't need the guilt and I don't need you

persuading me to walk away or go home.

I've come too far.

ROBERT. I won't say another word.

> *(Pause.)*

Show me the autograph.

HE. No.

ROBERT. Why'd you get his autograph?

HE. Go away!

ROBERT. You could have got him.

HE. I couldn't. Not then.

ROBERT. You didn't wanna. He was a nice guy.

He was polite. That stumped you, huh?

Caught you off-guard. Trying to get that photographer

to stay so you wouldn't do it.

You lost your nerve.

HE. He was polite.

He put the date next to his autograph.

They never do that. He asked me how I was.

Whether I wanted anything else.

(Pause.)

ROBERT. But he wasn't *real*.

You know he wasn't *real*.

HE. What do you mean?

ROBERT. He got in the limo pretty fast, huh?

Didn't hang around.

HE. So?

ROBERT. Did he look at you when he asked how you were?

Did he look into your eyes?

That's all I'm saying.

I mean, do you really think he gave a damn?

HE. I don't know.

ROBERT. If he comes back, you think he'll recognize you?

HE. Maybe.

ROBERT. Why? You're dimes and cents.

He has dregs like you hang round here all the time.

HE. He asked me how I was.

He didn't have to do that.

ROBERT. Well, what do you think he said to his little Geisha when

he got in the car?

HE. Stop using that word, will ya? So they're both...

ROBERT. What? Japanese?

HE. Yes. Who cares? You didn't used to be like this.

So...so...

ROBERT. What?

HE. You used to help me!

ROBERT. Wo-ah, wo-ah. I was just joking, buddy.

Just trying to have some fun. Lighten up.

HE. He probably asked her if she was okay.
Something like that.

ROBERT. Or maybe he remarked on how fat you are.

HE. It's the coat. I'm bundled up.

ROBERT. Something like, "Hey Yoko, check out the fat
cat in the hat."
Something like that.

HE. He wouldn't have said that.

ROBERT. How'd you know? Do you know him intimately?

HE. I met his son and their nanny earlier on today.
I shook their hands.

ROBERT. I saw. Cute kid.
You sick fuck.

HE. I should go back to the hotel.

ROBERT. Good idea. The Sheraton's expensive.
Get your buck's worth.

HE. Yeah.
Yeah. I'm going back to the hotel.

ROBERT. But on the other hand...

HE. What?

ROBERT. Well, it'd be kinda cowardly wouldn't it?
And let's face it, kinda typical.

HE. What do you mean?

ROBERT. It'd just be another of your fads.
Something else where you didn't follow through.
But hey, why not? Add it to the list.
Your faith, your music...your comedy skits –

HE. Look –

ROBERT. ...Your comedy skits, your painting, your art
collecting,
your missionary work –

HE. Okay, I get –

ROBERT. ...Reading all the books in Honolulu Library,
married to Gloria

but spending the night with prostitutes... Come on,
man.

When are you going to take a stand?

Why don't you be *somebody*?

HE. Okay, okay. I got it!

I'll stay.

> *(Silence. **HE** shivers in the cold.)*

ROBERT. Pretty shitty though.

Pretty shitty thing to do.

> *(Pause.)*

You'll piss a lot of people off, you know?

Hurt a lot of people. That's for sure.

It's really a horrible idea when you look at it.

You won't be a somebody at all.

You'll be famous for being a nobody, if anything.

> *(A beat.)*

Ugh.

HE. I think I need to sleep on it.

There's always tomorrow.

ROBERT. Always tomorrow.

Didn't he say he was bigger than Jesus?

Remember when he said that?

HE. He said they were.

The four of them.

And he took it back.

ROBERT. Remember how that made you feel.

HE. He was misquoted.

That was all.

It was a long time ago.

ROBERT. "Famous for being a nobody."

HE. I need a cab.

I'm gonna get a cab.

ROBERT. Of course...

HE. What?

ROBERT. Of course, that'll be sheep.

That's what the sheep will say.

But who cares what they think?

If it's all for the greater good, then you're in the right.

You just answered the call. We both know that.

You are The Catcher in the Rye.

You've got to protect the innocent, the new generation, those who don't know any better.

Save them from falling off that damn crazy cliff, just like you.

> (Silence. **ROBERT** turns around and looks up and around.)

Jeez, what a humble guy.

This place is like a castle in some fairy tale or something.

> (Turns back, laughs briefly.)

What a phony.

HE. It's not like he owns the whole building.

Leonard Bernstein lives here too...and Lauren Bacall.

ROBERT. No kidding? He's still a phony.

He lied to you. He lied to everyone.

All that stuff about peace and love and no possessions, it was all phony. You just have to turn around.

HE. I took it too seriously. That's all.

He didn't lie it was just music.

That's all it was.

ROBERT. Leading young folks astray like that.

Shame on him.

All sex and drugs, marching for peace when they should be

concentrating on their grades in school. Look where it's got you?

Shame on him.

He was just selling something else. He's just a rich bastard
like all the other phony rich bastards that run the world.

HE. Nah, it was just –

ROBERT. SHAME ON HIM!
You got duped. Plain and simple.
Chasing fairies right off the edge of the cliff,
meantime he's laughing all the way to the bank.
Welcome to the eighties. You're twenty-five now.
Not a kid anymore. Where's that leave you?

    (**HE** *shivers.*)

    (*Quietly, but enough volume for* **HE** *to hear him.*) "The phony must die says the Catcher in the Rye
The Catcher in the Rye says the phony must die,
John Len-non, John Len-non
The phony must die says the Catcher in the Rye
The Catcher in the Rye says the phony must die."

    (**HE** *shivers again.*)

Are you cold?

HE. Yeah.

ROBERT. It ain't Honolulu, that's for sure.
Could you have lived here?
If you had your time again?

HE. No-uh. Too loud. Too dirty. Too cold.
The place is full of freaks.

ROBERT. Sure.
I can see that.

HE. I don't know, you know?
It's getting late.

ROBERT. You're not going all yellow are you, Mark?
Don't tell me that you're going all yellow.

    (*A beat.*)

Well, hello.

(A sound of an approaching car is heard. They both look in that direction.)

ROBERT. Jackpot. I think this is it.
Showtime.

HE. I can just go. I really can. Fly back to Hawaii tomorrow. Back to Gloria. Get back with Christ. Get better. She loves me. He loves me. She'll help me with that. She's the best thing that's happened to me.

*(The sound of car doors shutting. **ROBERT** and **HE** watch the new arrivals as they pass them by and continue to watch them.)*

ROBERT. Here we go.

HE. No.

ROBERT. Here we go. Here we go. Here we go.

HE. I don't wanna.

ROBERT. Now come on! You came all this way! Finish it!

HE. No! Please!

ROBERT. Do it. Do it. Do it. Do it. Do it.

*(**HE**'s hand moves toward his pocket.)*

You can have him now!

(Backs away toward exit.)

PUT YOUR HAND IN YOUR POCKET!
HE'S YOURS! HE'S MINE! YOU PROMISED!
YOU BASTARD! PHONY BASTARD! YOU PROMISED!

*(**ROBERT** exits. **HE** pulls out a gun from his coat pocket. He drops into a combat stance. Blackout.)*

Revelation

GLORIA. Mark has this dream. A recurring dream.
He tells me about it when I go and visit him,
and now I have it too. We're back in Honolulu,
we're older now, and at the break of dawn, he wakes
up beside me, and as I sleep, he slips quietly out of
bed as not to wake me. He tiptoes across the carpet
and out into our living room and in the soft shadows
and silence, he recalls something horrible that almost
happened a long time ago. Just to make sure it didn't
happen, just to reassure himself, he looks over at the
picture frame hung up on the wall...

> (HE *appears in a spotlight. He is wearing
> pajamas and his hair is slightly ruffled. He
> walks a couple of paces downstage and then
> stops.*)

...he walks over to it and reads the words
"Double Fantasy." But with just the street light coming
in
through the window, he can barely see the
scrawling signature that's under it...

> (HE *puts on his glasses.*)

...then it comes into focus.
"John Lennon, December 1980."

> (*Brief silence.* HE *turns around and walks
> upstage, the lights fade on* HE.)

Now he wants to go back to bed and lie down
close next to me. Just him, my husband, and me,
his sleeping wife. Just the way it started out.
When it was just the two of us...

> (*Lights fade on* GLORIA.)

End of Play

ı